Hephaestus and the Island of Terror

Don't miss the other adventures in the Heroes in Training series!

Zeus and the Thunderbolt of Doom

Poseidon and the Sea of Fury

Hades and the Helm of Darkness

Hyperion and the Great Balls of Fire

Typhon and the Winds of Destruction

Apollo and the Battle of the Birds

Ares and the Spear of Fear

Cronus and the Threads of Dread

Crius and the Night of Fright

COMING SOON:

Uranus and the Bubbles of Trouble

Hephaestus and the Island of Terror

Joan Holub and
Suzanne Williams

Aladdin
New York London
Toronto Sydney New Delhi

This book is a work of fiction. Any references to historical events, real people, or real places are used fictitiously. Other names, characters, places, and events are products of the authors' imagination, and any resemblance to actual events or places or persons, living or dead, is entirely coincidental.

ALADDIN
An imprint of Simon & Schuster Children's Publishing Division
1230 Avenue of the Americas, New York, NY 10020
First Aladdin hardcover edition August 2015

Also available in an Aladdin paperback edition.

Jacket designed by Karin Paprocki
Interior designed by Mike Rosamilia
The text of this book was set in Adobe Garamond Pro.
Manufactured in the United States of America 0715 FFG
2 4 6 8 10 9 7 5 3 1
Library of Congress Control Number 2015908991
ISBN 978-1-4814-3510-9 (hc)
ISBN 978-1-4814-3509-3 (pbk)
ISBN 978-1-4814-3511-6 (eBook)

For our heroic readers:
Andrew M., the Andrade Family, Julia A., Kiki V.,
Emily G., Denny S., Christine D-H and Kenzo S.,
Sven S., Tait L., Sam R., Sophia O., Luke O.,
Harper M., Harrison T., Ariel S., Colin S., Caitlin R.,
Hannah R., Kiana E., Aspasia K., Tiffany W.
and Justin W., Heather H., Evilynn R., Alexa M.,
Ahalya S. and Sahara S.,
and you!
—J. H. and S. W.

Contents

Hephaestus and the Island of Terror

Greetings, Mortal Readers,

I am Pythia, the Oracle of Delphi, in Greece. I have the power to see the future. Hear my prophecy:

Ahead I see dancers lurking. Wait—make that *danger* lurking. (The future can be blurry, especially when my eyeglasses are foggy.)

Anyhoo, beware! Titan giants seek to rule all of Earth's domains—oceans, mountains, forests, and the depths of the Underwear. Oops—make that *Underworld*. Led by King Cronus, they are out to destroy us all!

Yet I foresee hope. A band of rightful rulers called Olympians will arise. Though their size and youth are no match for the Titans, they will be giant in heart, mind, and spirit. They await their leader—a very special boy. One who is destined to become king of the gods and ruler of the heavens.

If he is brave enough.

And if he and his friends work together as one. And if they can learn to use their new amazing flowers—um, amazing *powers*—in time to save the world!

CHAPTER ONE

Wake Up Already!

Early morning sunlight filtered through the trees as the ten most wanted outlaws in Greece ran along a wooded path. They were on a quest, heading for the coast of the Aegean Sea. And they knew that any minute the enormously tall King Cronus—the evil leader of the Titans—might pop up and attack them. His entire Crony army was searching for them, to take them prisoner.

Why? Because they were Olympian gods and goddesses! And even though they were all just human-size ten-year-olds, Cronus knew that these immortals would do anything to stop his dastardly plans to take over the world.

Zeus, a blue-eyed, dark-haired boy, stayed just ahead of the other nine immortals. As he ran, a worried expression on his face, he kept tabs on their surroundings. Since he was the leader of this bunch, he was always concerned for their safety. Keeping pace with him was his brother Poseidon, who shared the same dark hair but had eyes the turquoise color of the sea that he ruled.

And behind them, the rest of the gang jogged along. There were three other boys—Ares, Apollo, and Hades. And five girls in all—Artemis, Athena, Demeter, Hera, and Hestia.

"The goats are angry. Quick! Get the fig jam!"

Artemis mumbled. She was their weak link. She stumbled along at the back of the line, her sleepy eyes half-closed. Her twin brother, Apollo, held her arm, guiding her.

When blond-haired Hera turned to stare, Apollo shook his head in dismay. "She keeps talking in her sleep. Her dreams and thoughts must run very deep!" he explained, talking in singsong rhyme-speak as usual.

"Well, she's slowing us down," Hera said. She sounded a bit breathless from jogging along the rocky forest path.

"It's not her fault," said Apollo, panting too. "That sleeping potion the Titans gave her during our last quest still hasn't worn off."

"It's been seven days!" exclaimed Hera. "Is she ever going to wake up?"

"You know the answer," said gray-eyed Athena. Her aegis, the shield that she wore over her tunic, rattled as she scurried along. "Pythia said Artemis *can't* wake up till she finds her gold bow and silver arrows on the Island of Lemnos."

"And the sooner we reach the coast, the closer we'll be to the island," said Hestia.

"I know, but—" Hera began.

Zeus could hear them arguing behind him, and he sighed. "Chill out," he called back to Hera. "Quests are never easy, but we've got to follow Pythia's instructions just the same."

Pythia, the Oracle of Delphi, had been sending them on quests ever since Zeus had learned that he was an Olympian and not just a mortal boy. A prophecy foretold that the Olympians would overthrow King Cronus and the evil Titans someday. However, Pythia kept saying they weren't ready for that yet. Each of them needed to find their own magical object or weapon first, and there were still more Olympians to find too.

From beside Zeus, Poseidon looked back at the sleeping Artemis. She was falling farther and farther behind despite Apollo's support. "Stop the chickens!" she said, flapping her arms like wings.

"Maybe another squirt of water?" Poseidon suggested, lifting the trident he held. It looked like a pitchfork but was magical and could shoot water from the ends of its three pointy prongs.

"No!" called out Apollo, who had overheard. "There is no fun in being damp when you're outside and have to camp."

"What rhymes with 'you and your rhymes are annoying'?" Hera asked him huffily.

Apollo appeared to consider this. Rhymes were his specialty, especially the ones in songs. He was a talented musician. He could sing and also play the lyre, a stringed instrument that he carried slung across his back. "Well . . . ," he started to say.

Hera rolled her eyes. "Never mind," she muttered.

"Hold up," Athena hissed. Everyone came to a dead stop, panting as she pointed to a footprint in the dirt. "It's so big that it has to have been made by a Crony," she said. Though not as enormous as King Cronus, the Cronies were way bigger than the Olympians. In fact, they were as tall as trees!

Zeus looked over at Hera. "She's right. Can you use your feather to scout for King Cronus and his army?"

Nodding, Hera pulled her magical object, a peacock feather, from her belt. It was green and had blue and orange markings on the end that looked like an eye, so it was called the Feather of Eyes.

She held it in her palm and chanted, "Feather be my eyes for me, let me know if you spot a Crony."

"Lame-o," Artemis murmured sleepily.

She was right, thought Zeus. He would never say so to Hera, but her rhyme had kind of stunk. It had taken her a long time to find her feather, and she was quite proud of it. However, it would only follow commands spoken in rhyme. And though she might think otherwise, she didn't have the skill that Apollo did when it came to rhyming. Still, the feather obeyed her now and floated off.

Apollo grinned at Hera. "You know, I could help you with your rhyming if you want," he offered.

She glared at him and his sister. Before she could lash out at Apollo, Hestia piped up. "When your feather comes back, maybe you could tickle Artemis all the way awake," she suggested to Hera.

"Or I could try growing a remedy for her."

Demeter, the goddess of the harvest, touched the magical packet of seeds that hung from her belt.

"That'll take too long," Athena put in.

"True," said Demeter. "And it would be better to save the seeds for crops if we can." Just one of her magic seeds could grow enough food to feed a whole village. So she used them carefully, not wanting to waste them.

Zeus spoke up, whispering in case any Cronies were close. "The only solution for Artemis is to find her bow and arrows. Like Pythia said."

"But remember what else she said?" Poseidon whispered back. "That we'll have to fight off silver lines and gold dolls before we get to those arrows."

Hera giggled. "Sorry, but fighting lines and dolls doesn't sound scary at all compared to the battles we've faced on our other quests." In the past the Olympians had fought off some terrifying monsters—a three-headed dog, bird women with razor-sharp claws, weird warriors who hopped around on one foot—and more.

"Sometimes Pythia doesn't see things clearly, though," Zeus reminded her. "I wish we could be a hundred percent sure what we were going to be up against."

"Or even ninety percent," quipped Poseidon.

Just then the peacock feather flew back into Hera's hand. She looked into its orange eye and gasped. "There's a Crony up ahead, coming this way!" she exclaimed. "Just one, I think. He looks like a scout."

"Hide!" said Zeus, running for cover.

"Aw, come on. It's just one Crony. We can take him! Anyone up for a fight?" asked Ares, waving his spear. He was the god of war and was always eager for battle.

"No! He could sound an alarm and call up an army," argued Zeus. "We can't take that chance."

Disappointment showed in Ares's strange red eyes, but he didn't argue.

"Hurry!" said Hera. "He's getting closer."

"There's a clump of bushes over there," said Demeter, pointing. The Olympians hurried to take cover.

"All right," Zeus told the others. "Settle down and stay quiet."

"What if Artemis starts snoring?" Hera asked.

"Artemis! Where is she?" Apollo exclaimed, looking around suddenly. "I let go of her for half a second, and now she's gone."

Zeus peeked out from the bushes. There, not more than ten feet away, stood Artemis. "Frog jumped over the moon," she said softly. Shoulders drooping, she stood right in the middle of the path. She was asleep on her feet!

Crunch! Crunch! It was the sound of huge boots crossing the sandy soil. The Crony scout. He was coming closer. In seconds he would discover Artemis!

Hera elbowed Zeus. "Do something!"

CHAPTER TWO

It's Not Really Stealing . . .

Zeus leaped out of the bushes. He rushed over to Artemis, grabbed her by the arm, and half-dragged her to their hiding spot just in the nick of time.

From the bushes the ten Olympians watched the Crony scout appear through the trees. He looked fierce in his loincloth and metal chest armor, and he was bulging with muscles. In other words, he was dangerous!

"Who brought the carrots?" Artemis murmured through her haze of sleep.

Poseidon clapped a hand over her mouth before she could say anything more. Unfortunately, she bit his hand and he almost cried out. Fortunately, Hera clapped a hand over Poseidon's mouth to keep him quiet too. The other Olympians all held their breath as the Crony stopped and looked around. Would he search for them now?

Luckily, the Crony, didn't seem to think whatever he'd heard was important. Moments later he stomped on by. *Phew!* Zeus let out a breath of relief. When they couldn't hear the crunching of the Crony's boots anymore, the immortals stepped out of hiding.

"Ow!" Poseidon said at last, rubbing his hurt hand. But a few sprinkles of water from the pronged tips of his trident seemed to quickly ease his pain.

"Good. He's going inland, opposite from the way we're going to reach the coast," said Hera.

"So I guess the coast is clear," joked Hades. Unlike Artemis, he'd been pretty quiet up till now.

"Let's hope so," said Zeus. Just in case, he stayed alert. You never knew. An entire army of Cronies could surprise them when they least expected it.

Apollo nudged Zeus's arm as they started off on their journey again. "Thank you, mister, for saving my sister."

"Anytime," Zeus replied, and he meant it. Artemis was under a spell and meant no harm. And he had only done what needed to be done. No matter how dangerous, difficult, or scary the task, that was what Olympians did.

The words of his mother, Rhea, came back to him. *I know you will make good choices, Zeus. You and the other Olympians have made many good choices already. You are kind to one another and the mortals you meet. You help those in need.* She had told Zeus this when she'd appeared to him in the shadows during his recent battle with an important Titan named Crius.

When the huge Titan had teased him, Zeus had grown angry. Very angry. It was an anger like he'd never felt before—uncontrollable. He'd pinned Crius to the ground, holding one of his magical objects, Bolt, high and ready. It had sizzled with electric energy. His hand had trembled. He'd wanted to zap Crius, to destroy him with a massive blow from the daggerlike thunderbolt.

But the voice of his mother had stopped him.

Had losing control like that meant Zeus was as evil as King Cronus himself? He didn't want to be evil. But Zeus had learned on another quest that King Cronus was actually his father! Since then Zeus constantly worried that he might one day turn out as rotten as the king.

Rhea had told him not to worry, that he could make his own choices and did not have to end up like Cronus. His mother's words had made Zeus feel better. Still, sometimes his anger surged again, and he wondered if Rhea could have been wrong.

After some time passed, Poseidon took a deep breath. "Salt air!" he announced, breaking into a big smile. "We're close to the sea!"

When the Olympians heard this, they began running faster. Minutes later they came upon a busy dock filled with ships. Fishermen scurried about, loading and unloading their ships with baskets of goods. Beyond the ships the blue-green waters of the sea glittered in the morning sunlight.

"Keep an eye out for Cronies," Zeus warned as they made their way down to the docks.

"The brave Olympians were forced to flee, but at long last they reached the sea," Apollo sang happily.

"Hey, post a sign, why don't you?" grumped Hera.

"She's right," warned Zeus. "There could be Cronies around here somewhere, hiding. Or informants who'll tell them we were here. So it's best to keep quiet about being Olympians."

"Um, how exactly are we supposed to cross this sea to Lemnos anyway?" Hades asked, looking around. "We don't have a ship."

"Good question," Athena agreed. "Zeus, what's the plan?"

Zeus frowned, thinking. They didn't have any money to pay for passage to Lemnos. The only things they had of value were magical objects, and they couldn't part with them.

Ares spoke up before Zeus could answer. "Let's

storm one of the ships and take it for our own!" he cried, shaking his spear.

"We are *not* battling for a ship," said Zeus firmly.

"Yeah, battling for a ship would be an uphill . . . uh—*battle*—for sure," agreed Poseidon.

"Well, maybe we could cause a distraction and then just . . . borrow a ship," suggested Hestia.

Zeus frowned. "You mean . . . *steal* a ship?"

"Well, it's not stealing if we give it back after our quest," Hera reasoned. "I'm with Hestia on this."

The other Olympians murmured in agreement. They couldn't just ask the fishermen for help, thought Zeus. What if the fishermen were on the side of the Cronies? And the Olympians had to get to the Island of Lemnos somehow. He hated to admit it, but stealing—that is, *borrowing*—a ship might be their only option.

Zeus reached for the magical object tucked into his belt. "I guess I could use Bolt to create a thunderstorm as a distraction while we steal—um, *borrow*—a ship." He'd found his thunderbolt-shaped dagger in Pythia's temple. That had been way back before he'd met these Olympians and started on this epic journey. At Zeus's command Bolt could grow to five feet long and sizzle with the power of the heavens.

But before anyone could reply, a cry rose up among the fishermen. "Fire! Fire!" Some of them raced toward a nearby sand dune, while others grabbed buckets and filled them with water.

"What happened?" Zeus began. But then he noticed that Hestia was holding up her magical object, a long metal torch decorated with carvings. A bright flame danced in the shallow bowl atop it. She closed her eyes, and seconds later another small fire broke out on a sand dune near

the first one. More fishermen with buckets of water ran toward it.

"Now the coast really is clear," quipped Hades.

"Good job!" Athena told Hestia.

Hestia smiled and did a little happy dance. "I'm getting better at controlling the flame," she said proudly.

"While everyone's trying to put out the fires, we might as well grab a ship," said Zeus. Clearly, it had been Hestia's intention when she'd started the fires to draw the fishermen away so they could do just that! Zeus looked at Poseidon. "Which one? It'll need to fit ten of us."

As they ran along the dock, Poseidon scanned the ships. "There!" he called, pointing.

The ship he'd chosen for them had a large, wooden hull and a wide, white sail. Three long oars extended from each of the ship's sides. It wasn't the largest ship on the dock, but it was just right for their group.

They rushed for the ship and quickly climbed on board. Hades and Hera hoisted the sails. The other Olympians—except for Artemis—grabbed the oars and started to row. The ship pulled away from the shore.

Suddenly Poseidon tossed his trident overboard. It splashed into the sea. Then he jumped in after it.

"First one to Lemnos wins!" he yelled happily. Straddling his trident, he zoomed off. Streams of water magically gushed out of the three prongs at its back end, shoving him forward across the waves.

CHAPTER THREE

Sea Monsters!

As Zeus moved to the helm of the ship, he touched the oval stone disk he wore around his neck. "Chip, which way is the Island of Lemnos?" he asked it. Poseidon knew the seas well and was probably going in the right direction, but confirmation from Chip would be good.

An arrow appeared on the stone, pointing north. A tiny voice said, "His-tip ay-wip!"

Chip was another of Zeus's magical objects. Most of the time, symbols appeared on it when Zeus asked a question. But Chip also spoke his own special language, Chip Latin. It was kind of like Pig Latin, only you moved the first letter of each word to the end of the word and added "ip."

"Thanks, Chip!" Zeus said. "A little to the left, you guys!" he shouted to Hades and Hera. His brother and sister Olympians shifted the sails just as a wind picked up, sending the ship forward. Fifteen minutes later they caught up to Poseidon.

"Hey, Fishbreath! We're going to beat you!" Zeus teased.

Poseidon grinned, looking happy and wholly confident as he skimmed across the sea. "You wish! The sea is my element, Thunderboy. When I'm in the water, it's like my whole mind opens up. I feel like I can do anything. It's awesome!"

Zeus had felt that kind of awesome feeling before, when Bolt was in his hand, and the wind and rain of a thunderstorm whipped around him. But that was before he'd battled Crius. Before the awesome feeling had been tainted by evil creeping into his heart. He shuddered, wanting to forget.

Hades ran up to him, holding a basket filled with food. "Hey, I found some bread and sardines in the hull. Think we could borrow them, too?"

Zeus's stomach rumbled at the mention of food. "Sure. Poseidon can catch more fish to replace that food later. So, yeah, go ahead."

"Hooray! I'm so hungry, I would eat the shoe off a Crony's stinky foot!" said Hades.

"Ew!" said several of the girls. However,

they all knew he liked things stinky. In fact, when some of the Olympians had been trapped inside King Cronus's belly before Zeus had rescued them, Hades had actually been happy down there!

A few minutes later the Olympians were munching bread and sardines as the wind carried the ship to Lemnos. Even Artemis woke up enough to sleep-chew.

Zeus gazed upward. The sky was blue, the air was cool, and his belly was full.

"What a beautiful day. Things are going our way," Apollo sing-songed, echoing Zeus's thoughts.

"Don't jinx us!" Hera warned.

"Huh?" Apollo said. "There's no such thing as j—"

"Sea monsters!" Hades cried, jumping up from his seat near the sails. He was right! Two dragon-like heads had risen from the water by the bow of the ship.

One of the monsters was the turquoise blue of the sea, and the other was emerald green. Instead of ears there were fins on either side of each monster's head. And their teeth looked big enough and sharp enough to bite the ship in half.

"Monster attack!" Ares yelled, his red eyes blazing. He lifted his spear, poised to throw it.

"Wait! Don't hurt them!" Poseidon warned. He zipped between the sea monsters and the ship, riding on his trident.

"This ship holds my friends! You must let them pass safely," he commanded the monsters.

It worked! Recognizing him as the god of the sea, the monsters bowed their heads in awe. "As you wish, Lord Poseidon," the green monster rumbled in a deep voice.

"Wow. Impressive save, Bro," Hades called

down to him. "We were almost sea-monster food!"

Poseidon shrugged, but he was smiling proudly.

"Let us aid you on your journey," the turquoise monster offered. "Where are you headed?"

Zeus stepped forward. "To the Island of Lemnos," he told them.

Both monsters' dragon-like heads jerked back in alarm, and their fin-ears flapped wildly. "No way!" said Green. "You're on your own."

"We apologize, Lord of the Sea. But we are afraid. No one goes to that island," Turquoise told Poseidon.

"Why?" asked Poseidon.

"Yeah, what's the matter with the place?" Zeus asked.

"It's spooky and dangerous. Plus there's something very, very weird about it. You should stay well away," Green replied.

"Spooky?" echoed Apollo.

"Dangerous?" echoed Athena.

Demeter leaned over the rail, her eyes wide. "And what do you mean by 'weird'?" But the two sea monsters sank back into the sea without answering.

"Maybe we should do as they say and turn back," Hades said with a worried look on his face.

"Turn chicken, you mean?" Hera scoffed as their ship continued to speed over the waves toward the island. "We can't. This is our quest."

"Hera's right," Zeus agreed. "We'll have to see for ourselves what's there."

"The island may be spooky and weird, but I'm sure it's nothing to be feared," added Apollo.

Hera scowled. "There you go, jinxing us again!"

"Not everything I say can be a jinx, can it?" Apollo protested, but the Olympians all looked worried now. An uneasy silence fell over the ship as they sailed on.

After what seemed like days, they heard Poseidon call out. "Land ho!" Finally!

The nine Olympians on board all rushed to the bow to see an island ahead, shrouded in fog.

"What's that dark thing looming in the middle of the island?" Hestia wondered aloud.

Others made guesses. "A mountain?"

"A volcano?"

"A Titan?"

And then they heard it: *Boom! Boom! Boom!* "Is that someone—or something—playing the drums?" wondered Athena.

"Oh, good. Maybe the islanders like music," Apollo said hopefully. As they sailed closer, the sound became clearer.

"I don't think it's drums. It sounds like hammers hitting . . . metal," Ares remarked. Their ship ran aground about twenty yards from shore.

"There are two rowboats on board," Zeus said. "Let's split up and then meet onshore."

"How will we find one another in that fog?" Hera asked.

"I've got Bolt, and Hestia has her flame," Zeus replied. "We'll each go in a different boat and flash our lights if we get separated."

After lowering the boats to the water, Zeus, Hades, Athena, Apollo, and a sleepwalking Artemis climbed into the blue rowboat. Hera, Hestia, Ares, and Demeter took the gray one. Poseidon zipped off toward shore, riding on his trident alongside them.

CHAPTER FOUR

What the Oog?

Rowing to the island seemed to take forever. Zeus could hear Apollo next to him, singing softly. He wondered why the fog was so thick, like a big, white blanket covering the island. He couldn't even see when their boat hit the shore—he could only feel it.

Bump!

"Bolt, we need light," said Zeus, holding up his dagger. But nothing happened. The thunderbolt's usual glow didn't come to pierce through the fog. Though he continued to shake Bolt, no light shone from it. "That's odd," he said.

Hades and Athena climbed out of the boat after him, and then they helped Apollo with Artemis. "Foggy," Artemis muttered and then yawned.

"Dark and spooky. I like it," said Hades. He sniffed the air, his face breaking into a big smile. "It even smells like the Underworld." Hades was god of that dank place, which lay beneath the earth.

"Ew! You mean the Underworld smells like rotten eggs?" Athena asked, wrinkling her nose in disgust.

"Rotten to you, awesome to me," Hades replied, and Athena shook her head.

"Since your bolt isn't working, Hestia's torch

would be very useful about now," Apollo remarked.

"Yeah, where is she? And the others?" Zeus asked, looking around as they waited. "Hera? Hestia?" he called out.

There was no answer. Zeus grabbed Chip.

"Chip, take us to the other Olympians," Zeus said. Like with Bolt, nothing happened.

Before he could try again, Athena shrieked. "Look out!"

Whoosh! An arrow sliced through the air and whizzed past his ear. Zeus heard it splash into the water behind him. Through the fog three more arrows came at the five Olympians.

"Duck! Run!" Zeus yelled.

"Which one? You're confusing me!" Hades yelled back as an arrow flew over his head.

"Both!" Zeus cried. "Head to the right! The arrows are coming from the other direction."

Too panicked to think clearly, Zeus covered his head with his hands and raced into the fog. The four other Olympians were at his heels. After about a hundred yards he stopped, trying to catch his breath. The fog was thinner here and he could see Hades, Athena, Apollo, and Artemis around him. "I guess we're safe here for now," he told them.

Just then a line of warriors stepped toward them out of the fog. "Uh-oh," said Artemis sleepily.

Each held a drawn bow loaded with an arrow pointed right at the Olympians. Bare-chested and bearded, they looked ferocious.

Hades quickly put on his magical object, an invisibility helmet. But it didn't work. He stayed visible.

"Hey!" Hades complained. "There's something wrong with my helmet. I should be invisible, but I'm not!"

"Tell me about it," said Zeus. "Bolt and Chip won't work either. There's something about this island . . ."

"Droog-ee-ur-woo-pongs!" barked one of the warriors. At least, that was what it sounded like to Zeus.

"What the 'oog' did he say?" Apollo whispered.

"Ponged if I know," Zeus whispered back.

"Root noog!" a different warrior said.

"Droog themoo!"added another.

"*The moo?* Do they want us to find them a cow?" Zeus wondered aloud.

"Doubt it. I think they want noodles," said Hades. "Where are we supposed to get noodles at a time like this?"

"Droog-ee-ur-woo-pongs!" the first warrior repeated impatiently.

Athena's gray eyes lit up. "No! I think he's saying 'Drop your weapons'!"

"No way!" Hades yelled. "We'll be helpless. Let's fight them!"

Athena shot him a frustrated glance. "What? Are you Ares now?"

Zeus thought fast. His and Hades's magical objects weren't working for some reason. Athena had her Thread of Cleverness and the aegis. Still, their magic probably wouldn't work either. Apollo had no magical object and wouldn't be able to fight even if he'd had one, since he had to prop up his sister. Also, they were outnumbered.

Zeus dropped Bolt and held up his hands, but he kept Chip just in case the stone began working again. "See? We mean no harm."

The head warrior nodded. Reluctantly following Zeus's lead, Hades dropped his helmet, and Athena took off her aegis.

"We're doomed," said Apollo.

"Yeah. Maybe our objects' magic would've

started working soon. But now there's no way we can fight them off," Hades muttered, his hands in the air too.

Zeus felt a pang of regret. Had he done the right thing?

CHAPTER FIVE

Hef-es-tu-soo!

Their weapons seemed to amuse the warriors. One of the men put on Hades's helmet, and another tried to put the aegis on his head. A third tried to use the sharp tip of Bolt to pick his teeth.

Zeus felt Athena press something into his hand.

"I didn't give them my Thread of Cleverness," she whispered. "I'll use its magic to weave a large net so we can get away from these goons. Just hold on tight to your end."

It was worth a try, thought Zeus. Before he could nod, the warriors surrounded the five Olympians and began herding them forward. Zeus and Athena walked side by side, their hands close together. But as they walked, the thread didn't grow any longer, like it had before.

"What is going on?" Zeus whispered after they had gone inland from the shore a little way.

Athena frowned. "Either the thread's magic isn't working, or I forgot how to do it." With a sigh, she took the other end of the thread back from him.

"Those sea monsters were telling the truth. There's something weird about this island," said Apollo.

"Yeah, and I have a feeling we're going to find

out what that something is whether we want to know or not," said Hades.

Artemis giggled, which sounded kind of spooky in the fog.

Zeus could only hope the other five Olympians hadn't been captured as well. "Keep an eye out for the others," he whispered.

As they marched toward the center of the island, the clanging metal sounds they'd heard earlier grew louder and louder. Though the fog thinned out more and more around them as they kept walking, it still hung in the air like a wispy, smoky blanket. Zeus could see they were heading toward the large thing at the island's center that they had seen from the ship.

"It's a volcano!" said Athena. Fog flowed from its top in big plumes, then curled outward to hug the edges of the island like a doughnut.

"That's not a volcano. It's a fog-cano," said Hades.

"And what's that? A fog monster?" wondered Apollo as they passed a strange object. It was a metal box that sat on top of three metal legs. It was twice as tall as Zeus. Foggy smoke billowed out of a grate at the front of the box. A huge tube that looked like it might stretch all the way to the volcano snaked into the back of the box.

"It's some kind of . . . machine," Athena noted. "I think the steam from the volcano is being sent through the tube and then shot out of the box."

"So it's . . . funneled fog?" Hades asked.

Athena shrugged. "Something like that," she replied.

As they continued to walk along, they passed a second machine just like the first one. Only this one seemed to be heading for the trees nearby. It was walking on its three legs, and then it scurried right up the thick trunk! *Creak! Creak!* It was also attached to a long tube—longer than the one on the first machine—that snaked through the tree as the box clambered up . . . up . . . and up.

The Olympians craned their necks, and realized there were more of the strange boxes among the leaves, supported by the thick branches that jutted out.

"How are the boxes moving around and making fog?" Hades wondered.

Zeus frowned. "It must be magic. There's probably a Titan on this island."

"And we don't have our weapons," Hades said.

"They don't seem to be working, anyway," Athena pointed out. "Hmm. I wonder why a

Titan's magic would work here but ours doesn't."

"No idea," said Zeus. Facing a Titan without weapons would not be easy, he thought. "Where are you taking us?" he asked their captors in his most demanding voice.

"Toog ur leader-oo," one of the warriors answered.

"They're taking us to their leader," Athena translated.

The warrior next to her laughed. "Leader-oo!" he sang out in a high voice.

Apollo began to sing too. *"The heroes were marched to a fiery hill. Being scared to death was part of the thrill."*

He kept it up, but Zeus couldn't hear because the loud clanging ahead drowned Apollo out. They started up a slope toward the base of the volcano.

Then Hades gasped. "Awesome!" In front of

them loomed a huge bronze door covered with designs that looked like human skulls.

Two of the warriors approached the door and started pounding on it. "Hef-es-tu-soo!" they shouted. The other warriors took up the chant. "Hef-es-tu-soo! Hef-es-tu-soo!"

Hefestusoo? Is that the name of the Titan? Zeus wondered.

Suddenly the loud clanging they had been hearing as they'd marched along stopped.

The bronze door swung open. A voice shouted from inside. "Enteroo!"

CHAPTER SIX

In the Heart of the Volcano

A blast of heat hit the Olympians as the warriors led them inside. The door had opened into a hallway with a low ceiling. Both the walls and the ceiling were lined with bronze. This was no ordinary volcano. It was a building with rooms and halls and doors.

"Phew! It's hot in here," Artemis said, fanning her face with her hand. Zeus stared at her in surprise. It was the first complete sentence she had said in days that actually made sense! Her eyes were a little more open than usual, and she wasn't leaning on her brother. Maybe the potion was finally wearing off. Or was it something else?

The warriors marched their captives down the winding hall. Every time they passed another warrior, they all called out to one another. "Hullooo!"

Eventually the hall opened up into a big, high-ceilinged workshop. Here more bare-chested warriors hammered metals and used bizarro tools to create strange-looking wonders. There was a mechanical falcon made of black metal sitting on a perch, stiffly flapping its wings. And a round ball of metal with eight spidery legs was skittering across the floor. Not to mention the giant metal cages hanging from the ceiling with various other mechanical pets hanging inside them.

The Olympians gazed around in amazement. Zeus had never seen anything quite like it—and he had seen a lot of crazy things on these quests.

And then he noticed it. The very thing they'd come for! There, hanging on the back wall, were six fine silver arrows and a gleaming gold bow.

Suddenly Artemis perked up. "Mine!" she cried, and moved toward them. But one of the warriors pushed her back into line.

"Hey!" Apollo complained, pulling her away from them. He, Hades, Athena, and Zeus exchanged glances as they all moved into another hallway. Somehow, at some point, they had to get those arrows and that bow for Artemis.

After more marching, they found themselves standing in front of a new bronze door. Flanking it were two tall statues, both beautifully crafted. A silver lion sat on the left, and a snarling gold dog on the right. Zeus shivered when he looked at them. He knew they were only metal, but they looked as if they could spring to life and attack at any moment.

"Hephaestusoo! Hephaestusoo!" the warriors chanted. But Zeus noticed that none of them pounded on this new door like they had the first one. Instead they waited with growing excitement.

"What are we waiting for?" Hades whispered to Zeus.

Then they heard a sound. *Thump! Thump! Thump!* It came from behind the door. Hearing it, the warriors' chanting grew more excited.

Thump! Thump! Thump! The sound got louder . . . and closer.

"Think there's a Titan back there?" Apollo wondered aloud.

Zeus started to sweat, imagining the huge Titan that was about to appear from behind the door.

Athena leaned over to whisper to him. "Hold on a second. That door is normal-size."

Yeah, so how could a giant Titan fit through it? Zeus realized. He brightened a little.

As the door swung open, every warrior dropped to his knees and bowed to the figure who'd appeared. Zeus was astonished to see that it was only a boy! A boy about the same size and age as the Olympians. He was dressed all in black, with a silver belt around the waist of his tunic and shiny armor on his wrists. His thick, dark hair was slicked back with oil, and his brown eyes were flecked with gold.

But what *really* caught Zeus's eye was the cane the boy was leaning on. It was the coolest—and scariest—cane he had ever seen. Like the first door they'd entered, it was carved with skulls. These were way smaller, though, and the cane had a skull-shaped knob at the top.

"He sure is tiny for a Titan," Hades whispered to Zeus.

"I don't think . . . ," Zeus started to say.

Thwack! The boy struck the ground with his cane, and eyed the Olympians fiercely. "I am Hephaestusoo! Bow down toog me!" he demanded.

When they hesitated, the warriors yanked them down, forcing them to drop to their knees.

"Have you no respectoo?" the boy asked. "What brings yoog to my island?"

"We are on a quest," Zeus replied.

"Quest? You're just a bunch of kids!" The boy laughed. "What kind of a quest could you be on? Are you looking for your mommies?"

No more "oos" and "oogs," Zeus noticed. Now the boy was speaking in the same way as the Olympians. What was up with that?

"Are you a tiny Titan? Or a mini Crony?" asked Apollo.

The boy struck his cane against the floor again. *Thwack!* "That's a rude question," he said. "But I will answer it, because I do know something of Cronies. And I have an amazing story to tell. When I was very young, I was taken prisoner by Cronies. They stole me from my home and stashed me away on a ship."

A look of sadness crossed his face, and he glanced away for a moment. Then he shifted his cane to his other hand and went on.

"On the second night of our journey, a terrible storm struck," he said. "The ship crashed onto the rocky coast of this island. None of the Cronies survived. But I did . . . barely."

He glanced down at his leg, and Zeus guessed that it must have been hurt in the shipwreck. That would explain the cane.

"So you were captured by Cronies," Athena asked. "Do you know why?"

The boy shook his head. "It is my guess that they feared my greatness, for you can now see what I have become. A respected and powerful leader-oo!" He motioned to the warriors, who bowed even lower. But Zeus noticed that a few of those warriors rolled their eyes at one another even as they bowed.

The Olympians looked at one another as realization dawned on them. "He's no tiny Titan!" Apollo said.

"He's one of us!" Hades cried.

Zeus rose to his feet and announced the truth to the boy. "You're the *eleventh* Olympian!"

CHAPTER SEVEN

A Mechanical Mind

"You're Olympians?" the boy asked in surprise as Zeus's four companions also got to their feet. "You mean, like the ones King Cronus is all fired up about capturing and . . ." He drew a finger across his throat, indicating that the king meant them harm.

"Yes," said Zeus. "We're those Olympians. And you're one of us."

The boy laughed and replied, “Hmm. Hephaestus, of the Olympians! Or maybe I’m supposed to be your leader? Hephaestus, Leader of the Olympians. It has a nice ring to it.”

Of course, Zeus hadn’t told the boy he was going to lead them. They didn’t even know him!

“Although, I can’t say I’m surprised by this news,” the boy went on. “I’ve always known I wasn’t like other mortals. Apparently my special qualities are even more special than I realized. I’ll have to ask my subjects to start worshipping me extra hard now!”

At that, some of the warriors started to giggle. But a glare from Hephaestus shut down that laughter pretty quick, and they started stomping their feet and clapping instead.

Zeus couldn’t believe how this tiny kid could make those ginormous warrior dudes do whatever he wanted with just one look! He wondered if those warriors really liked worshipping this strange boy—and why they did it in the first place.

"Um, well, here's the thing," Athena said. "We need to ask you to leave this place and come with us. Maybe you could help us find our friends? They should be on this island somewhere."

"Yeah," Zeus went on. He started pacing back and forth in front of Hephaestus. "You see, there's this oracle. And ever since we found out we were Olympians, she sends us out on quests." He paused, waiting for the boy's reaction.

Hephaestus cocked his head, appearing interested. "Go on."

But before Zeus could continue, Hades jumped into the conversation. "We mostly fight horrible monsters and Titans on our quests. And we search for magical objects and weapons and stuff."

At the mention of magic, the warriors looked at one another, curious. One of the warriors, who had taken Bolt, tapped it against the head of another warrior, who was still wearing Hades's helmet. When nothing happened, they all chuckled and started chattering among themselves.

"And find other Olympians," said Athena, joining in. "Like how they found me. And once we collect enough magical weapons and Olympians, we'll be able to fight King Cronus and beat him and his soldiers once and for all."

The warriors went silent, looking toward their tiny leader.

The gold flecks in Hephaestus's eyes sparkled. "I see. So if the Olympians defeat the king, we'll rule the world instead of him?"

"I think that's the idea," said Zeus. "The details are never entirely clear, because Pythia's spectacles fog up, and then she can't see into the future all that well. She's the oracle I was telling you about."

In spite of their attempts to convince him, Hephaestus looked doubtful. "Let me think about it," he said finally. "It's great here. I've got the perfect workshop, and besides, I like being worshipped by all these islanders. I mean, who wouldn't? Still, ruling over more than just this one island is pretty tempting."

This set the warriors to murmuring. They shot the Olympians dirty looks.

"Why exactly do all these guys worship you?" Athena asked.

"That's another rude question, but I'll answer this one too, because the answer is interesting," replied Hephaestus. "It's because of my brilliant mechanical mind! I'm a whiz with metalworking."

"We saw some of your work in the shop," said Apollo. "It's amazing, but why do they care so much about a bunch of metal toys?"

"There's more. Let me show you," said Hephaestus. He twirled his cane like a baton, then pointed it down the hallway. "Walk with me," he said. He set off, striding swiftly, despite his limp.

Without another word he led them farther down the hall. His minions followed too, bowing the whole way. When they all reentered the workshop, Hephaestus waved his cane and bellowed at the workers and minions. "Sintians!"

"What's a Sintian?" Apollo whispered to Zeus.

Overhearing, Athena whispered back, "Must be what the people who live here are called?"

"You are all dismissed-oo!" Hephaestus ordered,

twirling his cane. Unfortunately, he lost control of it and it accidentally flew out of his hands. *Smack!* It knocked one of the workers in the head.

"Oops! My bad," Hephaestus said. The worker scowled at him. But then he looked a little scared and bowed low.

"Wait! Our magical objects," Athena called out. "Your warriors took them, and we need them back."

"Done!" said Hephaestus. "But the Sintians had already hurried out before anyone could ask what they'd done with the objects. "Great," said Hades, shooting Zeus a glance full of blame. "We may have lost our objects forever!"

Just then the mechanical bird flew over the Olympians' heads and landed back on its perch. Hephaestus smiled. "One of my first creations. Pretty good, right?" he boasted. "You see, after I crashed onto this island, the Sintians found me on the shore. I wasn't sure if they were going to help or hurt me, but I felt like they needed me. I mean, they already knew how to use fire to soften and bend metal to make things, but their metalworkers weren't very skilled or creative."

"So they didn't know how to make all this stuff?" Athena asked.

"No way. I taught them. As soon as they handed me a hammer, I just knew what to do with it, somehow. I could hammer metal into all kinds of shapes. Then I discovered how to connect pieces to make weirdly amazing creatures, and to make them move, too."

His eyes shone. "When the Sintians saw what I could do, they were in awe, of course. They made me their leader. They thought my inventions were magic. Before I came, Cronies used to attack them all the time. But I promised them that my inventions would keep Cronies away. Now the Cronies never come near this island. Do you know why?"

Zeus thought he knew. "It's those three-legged boxes that make the fog so thick near the shore, right? They help make the island look extra-spooky with the steam from the volcano, and scare everyone away."

Hephaestus nodded. "And any enemy who did set foot here would be swiftly defeated by my other creations," he bragged. He pointed to a large ram-shaped metal animal still under construction. Two sharp, fierce-looking metal horns spiraled from its head.

"My mechanical creatures are not only cool and quirky. They're also deadly," Hephaestus explained happily. "Once it is finished, this ram could take down a line of Cronies in mere seconds."

"Pretty impressive," admitted Athena.

"But don't you see, that's exactly why we need you to come with us. None of us knows how to make weapons like yours," said Zeus. "Each of us has our own special skills. Together, we make a great team."

"Yeah. Wait till you see what I can do with a bow and arrow," said a girl's voice from behind them.

Zeus and the others spun around. It was Artemis! While everyone had been focused on the ram, she'd crossed the room and taken the gold bow and silver arrows down from the wall. Now she held the bow in her hands and was pulling an arrow back, looking ready to shoot.

"You're awake!" Apollo cried.

"Finally," Hades said happily. "Maybe now Hera will stop grumbling."

"Dream on," said Apollo.

"Unhand those!" Hephaestus said angrily.

Artemis shook her head. Instead of obeying him, she sent an arrow across the room. *Boing!* It went straight into the eye of a metal bull. "Bull's-eye!" she crowed.

"Pythia said you would only wake up when you had your gold bow and silver arrows. She was right!" cheered Apollo.

"Nuh-uh. That bow and those arrows are mine," Hephaestus protested. "I made them!"

"Sorry, Heffoo. You made them, but they were meant for me all along," said Artemis. "They're mine now. Right, Zeus?"

"Yep," Zeus told her. "We came for them and for a new Olympian. Now that we have both, let's all get going."

"You know, maybe I will come with you," said Hephaestus, seeming to decide it was okay for Artemis to keep the bow and arrows after all. "I've always wanted to work with lots of gold and silver. There's not much of that around here. Mostly it's bronze or iron. I bet there are more precious metals where you come from. Besides, you need a good leader. One who doesn't just turn your weapons over to a bunch of warriors and leave you defenseless."

"We already have a leader. Zeus," Hades said loyally.

"You're our leader?" Artemis said, staring at Zeus in surprise. "Did you really give up everyone's weapons without a fight?" She gripped her bow and arrows tightly as if worried he'd offer them to the next Sintian who walked by.

Zeus opened his mouth to defend himself and his decision, but Hephaestus was quicker to speak. "Soft, bro, soft," he said, shaking his head at Zeus in disgust.

"I am not soft!" But Zeus saw Artemis and Apollo exchange doubtful glances. That hurt.

Then he looked at Athena and was alarmed to see that her eyes were wide with fear. Turned out that her fear had nothing to do with her opinion of his leadership skills, however. "Um, didn't that silver lion and gold dog used to be by the throne room?" she asked, slowly pointing toward the door.

The lion and dog now blocked the entrance to the workshop. Though the animals weren't moving, the lion's green jeweled eyes and the dog's glittery red eyes both gave off an eerie glow.

"Uh-oh. I think my pets may have figured out that I'm planning to leave and become your leader," Hephaestus said. "My pet creatures and I are exceptionally connected."

He turned to the lion and dog. "Here, kitty, kitty. Here, doggie. I command you to . . ."

Before he could finish, the silver lion and gold dog sprang to life. With a mighty mechanical roar and a threatening growl, they pounced!

CHAPTER EIGHT

Awesome Artemis!

The Olympians took off running to all corners of the workshop, taking cover where they could.

"*Silver lines and gold dolls.* Pythia's warning!" Zeus yelled, diving behind the ram statue.

"But as usual, she muddled things a bit," added Apollo from behind a column.

"Yeah!" said Athena from behind a vase. "It wasn't lines and dolls, but *lions* and *dogs*!"

With a mighty roar, the lion opened its huge jaws, revealing a mouth of sharp silver teeth. *Grr!* growled the gold dog. It had long fangs and a mouth big enough to gobble an Olympian in two bites!

"Stop! I command you!" Hephaestus yelled as the two mechanical beasts charged again and again. He pointed his cane-staff at the creatures, but they took no notice.

"They're not listening to you!" yelled Athena.

"Is there some other way to make them stop?" Zeus asked.

"Well, no. Because I, uh, made them unstoppable," Hephaestus replied.

Artemis aimed an arrow at the silver lion as it began to stalk her and Apollo. "Do they have any weak spots?" she yelled.

"Maybe where the head and the neck connect!" called Hephaestus. "There are gears between them that an arrow could jam."

As the mechanical lion roared again, Artemis sent her arrow flying. *Zzzpt!* It lodged in the lion's silver neck, and sparks shot into the air. Luckily that slowed the lion down a bit.

"Awesome, Artemis!" Athena cheered.

Without wasting time, Artemis shot next at the mechanical dog. Her arrow nailed it right in the neck too. This slowed the beast down, but unfortunately didn't stop it.

"You guys get out of here!" she cried. "I'll keep these two at bay and catch up later!"

Zeus hesitated, but Artemis had a steely look in her eye that told him she was going to be fine.

"All right!" he called back, while glancing around the workshop one last time. And there, strewn on a table at the far end of the workshop, were the Olympians' magical objects.

"Guys! Over there!" Zeus cried, running toward the table. He picked up Bolt. "Bolt, large!" he commanded. But nothing happened!

"If that's a magical object, it won't work here," Hephaestus told him. "The volcano puts sulfur into the air," he explained, "and that drains the magic from stuff—except for stuff made from the metal on this island."

"Just like in the Underworld," added Hades. "We've got lots of sulfur there, too." After shoving on his helmet, he started to grab every spear and sword in sight.

"Hey!" Hephaestus protested. "What're you doing? Those aren't yours!"

"If our magical weapons won't work, we're gonna need some help to get out of here," Apollo pointed out, grabbing weapons too.

Hephaestus nodded. "All right then. Everyone, take what you can! Then follow me to the exit!"

Zeus frowned in frustration—he'd just been

going to say the same thing! But Hephaestus took the lead, motioning with his cane toward the weapon-strewn worktables.

As they headed for the exit, Zeus looked back at Artemis. The silver lion was on its side, its legs still in motion. The mechanical dog plodded forward slowly, dragging one of its gold feet behind it. Artemis let another arrow fly, and this one must've hit the gears inside the dog's neck. Sparks shot out, and the dog slowed to a stop.

"Wow, those arrows really are magic!" Hades remarked.

"That wasn't magic. That was skill," Artemis said proudly. "C'mon. I'm finished here. Let's get going, you guys!" she called.

"Yeah, let's make a run for the ship," said Apollo.

"You have a ship?" Hephaestus asked.

"Yes," said Zeus. "So are you coming with us?"

Hephaestus looked around his workshop. "I don't know. I'm still thinking about it," he said. "But I'll at least help you get out of here. C'mon."

The Olympians left the workshop and dashed down the long hallway that led out from inside the volcano. Artemis pushed open the door at the entrance to the volcano, and they ran outside. The Sintian guards gave them curious looks, but they bowed their heads when they saw their leader-oo.

Hephaestus stopped and looked at the guards. Then he looked at the volcano. "I'll miss this place," he said, sounding a little sad. Then he turned his gaze toward the Olympians. "But there's something about being with you all that feels right."

"Because you're an Olympian," Zeus reminded him.

"And also, you've been stuckoo on an islandoo for a long time with only beardedoo guys who talkoo funny and bowoo down to you," Hades said, and then laughed. "That's gotta get boring after a while."

Hephaestus took a deep breath. "I can see that it is my destiny to take my rightful place as an Olympian. Besides, you need a leader," he declared. "I am coming with you!"

CHAPTER NINE

Boom!

"A new Olympian we have *found-oo*. Now we're surely glory *bound-oo*!" cheered Apollo.

Hephaestus grinned. "I like the sound of that." He and Apollo high-fived.

"Let's get to the ship before any more of your creatures come to life and try to attack us," Zeus urged. He was a little jealous of how quickly the new Olympian was bonding with everyone.

They hurried back toward the shore. Just as before, the fog grew heavier and thicker as they made their way to the rowboats.

"We'll never find the others in this blanket of gray," Zeus complained.

Hephaestus found the nearest Sintian and poked him with his cane. "Stop the fog machines," he ordered.

Zeus slapped his forehead. "Right! The fog!"

The worker bowed and hurried off to do Hephaestus's bidding. Moments later the hum of the machines stopped, and the blanket of fog that hovered over the island began to vanish. When the group reached the shore, the fog was thin enough that Zeus saw Hera, Hestia, Demeter, Poseidon, and Ares waiting for them by the rowboats.

"We got lost in that weird fog and decided we'd better just wait for you to turn up," Hera explained. Spotting Hephaestus, her blue eyes grew wide. "Who's this?"

"Greetings, fellow Olympians!" he said, spreading his arms wide. "I am Hephaestus, your new leader."

Hera looked at Zeus. "Is he serious?"

"Well, let's talk about it later," Zeus answered. "I think it would be a good idea to get off this island as quickly as possible."

Ares ran up to Hades, Athena, and Apollo, whose arms were filled with weapons. "Oh man, look at all this cool booty! Is it ours?" he exclaimed, picking up a shiny silver shield.

"It is now, bro," said Hades. "Let's load the rowboats."

Hephaestus eyed the ship out in the water. "It's bigger than I thought it would be. I think there's room for some more of my stuff." He walked over to the nearest fog machine and fiddled with it. "Fetch more weapons," he told it. Immediately the machine took off on its three legs, climbing back up toward the volcano, its long tube automatically trailing behind.

Hades, Ares, Athena, and Artemis loaded the two rowboats, and then they, Hestia, and Demeter jumped into them and headed to the ship. "Back for you in a few, after we pack this loot aboard the ship," Artemis called back to the Olympians still on shore.

"So the spell on Artemis wore off," Hera remarked to Zeus as they watched the rowboats glide away.

Zeus nodded. "Yeah. We found her gold bow and silver arrows."

"What about the silver lines and gold dolls?" Hera asked.

"Oh, we found those, too," he answered. "Except it was a silver *lion* and a gold *dog*.

And they came to life, thanks to the amazing mechanical skills of this guy here." He pointed toward Hephaestus, but he tactfully didn't add that the lion and dog had attacked the Olympians.

Hephaestus, who'd been talking with Apollo and Poseidon, overheard and came over. "By 'this guy' he means me, the ruler of this whole island," he said, motioning with his cane, and accidentally whacking Hera in the process.

"Ow!" she muttered. "Watch it with that thing. And just because you can rule an island doesn't mean you can rule us," Hera said, rubbing her shoulder with a frown.

"Of course," Hephaestus replied. "Are you loyal to Zeus, then?"

"Not necessarily," Hera answered, which Zeus wasn't surprised to hear. "I was just thinking that if there were going to be a new leader, it might be somebody more experienced with fighting Titans. Somebody like me, maybe."

Zeus rolled his eyes. *Great! Now* everybody *wants to be leader,* he thought. And then he noticed more of the three-legged walking machines coming down the path. A group of Sintians was following them. The platform on top of each machine was loaded with weapons and pieces of metal.

"To the ship!" Hephaestus ordered the machines. They obeyed his command, wading through the water toward the ship, while balancing the spoils they carried. Hades, Ares, Athena, and Artemis passed them, returning with the rowboats.

"Looks like we can head out now," Zeus said.

Hephaestus turned to the Sintians. More and more of them had started to gather on the shore, curious about the commotion.

"My loyal subjects!" Hephaestus called out to

them. To fully capture their attention, he waved his cane around, accidentally bonking *himself* in the head this time.

"Ow! Ahem," he said, wisely lowering his cane and rubbing his head. "The time has come for me to leave you. I must follow my destiny."

At this announcement, the Sintians began to murmur among themselves.

"Leader-oo must noot leave-oo!" one of the warriors shouted.

"Oog! Oog! Oog!" agreed the others, raising their voices in a chant.

"Calm down!" ordered Hephaestus, but the Sintians did not listen. Instead the warriors among them drew their weapons.

"A fight!" Ares cheered, shaking his spear.

"Our magical weapons don't work on the island," Zeus told him. "But they might work once we're offshore. And the weapons from

Hephaestus's workshop are already on board. To the ship!"

The Olympians ran for the rowboats—except for Hephaestus, who refused to believe the Sintians would disobey him.

"Droog-ee ur woo-pongs now!" he thundered, but his demand only made them angrier. An arrow whizzed past his face. "How dare you!" he yelled, slamming his cane into the ground.

"Groog leader-oo!" one of the warriors shouted. At that, a massive Sintian scooped Hephaestus up.

"Put me down!" Hephaestus demanded.

Artemis stood up in the rowboat. "I got this," she said confidently, and aimed an arrow at the warrior. "One arrow in the backside coming right up." Unfortunately, Hephaestus was kicking and flailing his arms, making it difficult for her to zero in on the Sintian.

"Careful!" Athena said worriedly.

Artemis's eyes narrowed, and she let the arrow fly.

Whoosh! Her silver arrow whizzed through the air and poked the Sintian—right in the behind.

"Oog!" the Sintian cried, dropping Hephaestus. The boy used his cane to pull himself up and then quickly climbed onto one of his three-legged machines, which was just then walking past. "To the ship," he told it.

By now the other Olympians had reached the ship. They clambered aboard.

"Hurry, Hephaestus!" Zeus called out as they hauled up the rowboats too. Hephaestus might be annoying, but they needed every Olympian they could find.

The Sintians let out angry shouts and shot a swarm of arrows toward their leader.

Once all except Hephaestus were on board, Artemis immediately knelt down and shot even more arrows toward the Sintians. One by one she knocked the weapons right out of their hands.

"Quick! We need to recharge our magical objects!" Hera yelled.

The Olympians formed a tight circle on the deck of the ship. Zeus held up Bolt and Chip. Poseidon held up his trident, and Athena did the same with her aegis and Thread of Cleverness. The others also thrust their objects and weapons high. Hades raised his helmet. Demeter, her bag of seeds. Hestia, her torch. Ares, his spear. And lastly, up went Hera's peacock feather.

As the objects came together, meeting high in the air between the Olympians, the objects all began to glow softly. Their magical light grew brighter . . . and brighter, until . . .

Boom! A mighty charge of energy surged through all of the objects, rocking the ship with its power. Brought together, their immortal magic always became far stronger. And Bolt glowed brightest of all! Its magic was working again!

At last the Olympians broke apart. Hearing a grinding sound, they raced to the side of the ship.

Creak! Creak! The three-legged machine Hephaestus was riding on was almost to the ship. Apparently its tripod legs had extended since its platform stayed above the water. There were so many Sintian arrows stuck in it now that it looked like a porcupine! It teetered left, then right, acting dizzy. Then it toppled over backward! *Splash!* Hephaestus fell into the water too.

"I've got this!" Poseidon cried. Quickly he tossed his trident into the sea, jumped down onto it, and zipped across the water to the rescue.

Meanwhile the Sintians charged into the sea, their arrows continuing to fly toward Hephaestus—and now Poseidon. "They're not going to make it. Do something!" Hestia urged Zeus.

He held Bolt high. "Large!" he yelled. At his command, the weapon grew to a sizzling supercharged lightning bolt five feet long. He aimed it at the Sintians, who were firing at Hephaestus and Poseidon.

Zap! In a burst of jagged light, Bolt shot from Zeus's hand. It struck some of the low plants along the shoreline. As they sizzled and then turned black, Bolt zoomed back to Zeus.

"Back off or else!" Zeus warned the Sintians. "Bolt's electricity will fry you like fish!"

A cry rose up from the Sintians. "Boots! Boots!" they chanted, punching angry fists in the air.

"Do they really think boots will protect them from Bolt's electricity?" Athena wondered aloud.

But seconds later dozens of new Sintians

appeared on the island's shore, some of them carrying *boats*.

"This means war!" shouted Ares.

"No! Sure, I could unleash Bolt to fry every warrior on the beach. But Sintians aren't monsters or machines. They're mortal men. *Weird* men, but men just the same. Let's just get out of here while the getting is good!" Zeus shouted to the others.

Just then Poseidon and Hephaestus zoomed up to the ship on the trident. Ares and Demeter rushed over and helped pull them aboard.

Once he stood on deck, Hephaestus looked back at the island. "Ingrates!" he yelled at the Sintians. Then his shoulders slumped and he spoke more quietly, and a little sadly. "I protected them and their island for years! I thought they worshipped me. Liked me."

Though Zeus hadn't known Hephaestus very long, he could kind of understand the Sintians' hostile feelings toward the boy. He could be pushy and he liked to brag. Still, Zeus put a hand on Hephaestus's shoulder. "You don't need them anymore. You have us."

Hephaestus brightened. "True! And you guys need me big-time. How fast can this ship move?"

"Depends on the wind," Zeus replied. "Why?"

The boy grinned mysteriously. "You'll see."

As he spoke, the whole island began to rumble. The ground shook, knocking some of the Sintians off their feet.

"What's happening?" Poseidon shouted.

"I suspected I might have to leave the island someday," Hephaestus said with a wicked grin. "So I made sure that no one would ever be able to steal my ideas and inventions. Wouldn't want the Sintians to use them to come after us and wage war, right?"

Zeus shuddered. He wasn't completely sure

what Hephaestus had up his sleeve, but whatever it was couldn't be good! "Set sail. And start rowing!" he shouted to the others.

Then he joined in, grabbing one of the long oars that could be used to get the ship moving when there was no wind. Meanwhile, Apollo, Athena, Hestia, and Artemis worked the sails. Waves crashed up against the ship, stirred by the trembling island.

"Faster!" Hephaestus hollered to them. He didn't bother to help, but only stared at the island with that same smug smile. Panicked, the Sintians scrambled to find safety.

Suddenly, bright orange sparks flew from the volcano. It rumbled and roared. And then . . .

BOOM! The volcano exploded in a shower of sparks and ash.

CHAPTER TEN

Find the Bubbles?

The ship moved away from the island, but not fast enough for Zeus. Sparks and ash were flying toward them. The Sintians took refuge in their boats, but made no effort to chase after the Olympians, fortunately.

"Faster!" Zeus yelled. The oars hit the water again and again, moving in a rhythm that pulled the ship slowly forward.

"I've got an idea," Poseidon told Zeus. Standing

in the bow of the ship, he held up his trident.

"Sea monsters! Come!" he called out, and his trident glowed. Within minutes the two monsters they'd met earlier emerged from the water in answer to his summons.

"We hear and obey you, Master," said Turquoise.

"Yes, even though you made us come to this weird island," Green grumbled.

Poseidon ignored his grumbling. "This place is bad news. I want you to get us out of here!"

Green nodded. "Told you so! Um, Lord Poseidon."

The sea monsters ducked underwater, and Zeus felt the ship begin to pick up speed. Thick, black smoke followed them from the island as the serpents pushed them out into the open sea.

"Where should we go from here?" Poseidon called back to Zeus.

Zeus hesitated. He really wanted to return

the stolen ship. But if the Cronies had gotten word of the theft, they might have guessed the Olympians had taken it. So going back to where they'd gotten the ship might not be safe.

While he was thinking, Hera spoke up. "I'll send out my feather to scout for a safe harbor," she said, and she held the Feather of Eyes in her palm. "Find us a place where we can hide, away from Cronies' prying eyes," she told it.

"Doesn't even rhyme," Apollo said, tsk-tsking as the feather floated away.

Soon the smoke was behind them, but they could still see black plumes billowing in the sky over the island. Hephaestus watched calmly.

"I know you were mad at those guys, but wasn't that kind of harsh?" Hades asked him.

Hephaestus shrugged. "They'll be okay. But they do not deserve my inventions. They proved that to me."

Hmm, thought Zeus. Hephaestus was clearly skilled when it came to metal inventions, but not so much when it came to people. Maybe he wouldn't be such a great leader after all.

Just then the feather returned to Hera. She looked into its eye. "There's a small island not far from here," she reported. "The sun is almost directly above it, so head west."

They changed course, and with the help of the sea serpents, they arrived at the small island just a few hours later. Then they rowed to shore in the rowboats and stepped out onto the beach.

"We can stay on the ship tonight, but let's check out the island first and make sure it's safe," Zeus told everyone. "We don't want to be attacked in our sleep."

"Very smart thinking, Zeus," said a voice.

Startled, Zeus glanced toward the place where the voice had come from, and saw a cloud of mist. A woman with long black hair and glasses appeared inside the mist.

"Pythia!" Zeus exclaimed, feeling glad to see her. "We completed our quest! We found another Olympian—Hephaestus. And Artemis got her bow and arrows and woke up."

Artemis held up her gold bow. "Yeah, thanks. Good to meet you."

Pythia smiled at her. Then her gaze scanned the group. "Well done, all of you."

Hephaestus stepped forward. "So are you the one who calls the shots in this group?" he asked. "I thought Zeus was supposed to be the leader."

"I see what the future holds," Pythia answered. "Well, not always clearly, but it is my duty to guide the Olympians. Zeus is their true leader."

Zeus was happy to hear Pythia say that. But part of him still wasn't sure if he felt worthy to be their leader anymore. He was always making

mistakes, it seemed. And when Hephaestus had called him "soft," some of the other Olympians had seemed to agree.

"And that brings us to your next quest," Pythia said. "You must find . . . the bubbles!"

"Find the bubbles?" Hera asked, confused. "Is that it?"

Pythia took off her glasses and cleaned the lenses with the edge of her white robe. "As usual, my spectacles are foggy," she replied. "That's all I can see. Ah, well." She faded into the mist.

Hephaestus turned to the others. "So *this* is how you get all your quests?" he said in disbelief. "A strange lady comes out of the mist and tells you to search for stuff, and you just go?"

"We found you, didn't we?" Zeus asked a little crossly. Hephaestus was really starting to get on his nerves! Maybe it wasn't a good idea to have him in the group after all, even if he was an Olympian.

"So what's the bubble plan, Bro?" Poseidon asked Zeus.

"*I* have a plan," Hephaestus butted in. "How about you all make me your leader? I've got lots of experience. Don't forget, I ruled a whole island."

"Thanks, but we barely even know you," Hestia said. "And Zeus has never steered us wrong."

"Thanks for the props," Zeus told her gratefully. Though it was a bit of an exaggeration to say that he'd *never* steered them wrong. Still, he appreciated her support.

Then Artemis spoke up. "I may have been half-asleep when we first landed on the Sintians' island," she said to Hestia. "But I do remember that when the Sintians asked us to drop our weapons, Zeus was like, 'Yeah, anything you want.'"

Hera raised an eyebrow at Zeus. "Really? You did that?"

Ares shook his head. "Wow, dude, that is weak."

"You weren't there," Zeus said in his own defense. "We were outnumbered. I made the best decision I could." And as he said it, he realized it was the truth.

"Zeus did great," Hades said, sticking up for him. "And anyway, Pythia says he's our leader. So I want to hear his plan for getting to the bubbles."

"I want to know Hephaestus's plan," countered Ares.

Suddenly the sky above them turned as black as night, plunging everything into total darkness!

"Well, somebody better figure out what to do," Hera said, sounding alarmed. "And fast. Because I have a feeling things are about to get really bad again. And I don't think we need an oracle to tell us that!"

She was right, Zeus thought. Springing into action, he whipped his dagger from his belt. "Bolt, on!" he ordered. Then, lighting the way, he led the others to the safety of some trees where they could wait to see what would happen next.